FOOTBALL FACTOR

TOUGH TACKLING

First published in 2013 by Wayland

Wayland
338 Euston Road
London NW1 3BH

Wayland Australia
Level 17/207 Kent Street
Sydney, NSW 2000

Series Editor: Victoria Brooker
Series design: Robert Walster and Basement68
Cover design: Lisa Peacock
Consultant: Dee Reid

A CIP catalogue record for this book is available from the British Library.
Dewey number: 823.9'2-dc23

ISBN 978 0 7502 7983 3

2 4 6 8 10 9 7 5 3 1

Printed in China

Wayland is a division of Hachette Children's Books, an Hachette UK Company
www.hachette.co.uk

FOOTBALL FACTOR
TOUGH TACKLING

Alan Durant and Andrew Chiu

WAYLAND
www.waylandbooks.co.uk

"Welcome back," said Kyle, the captain of Sheldon Rovers. He gave Ledley a thumbs up.

Four months ago, Ledley was badly injured. He had spent hours in the treatment room. Now he was back.

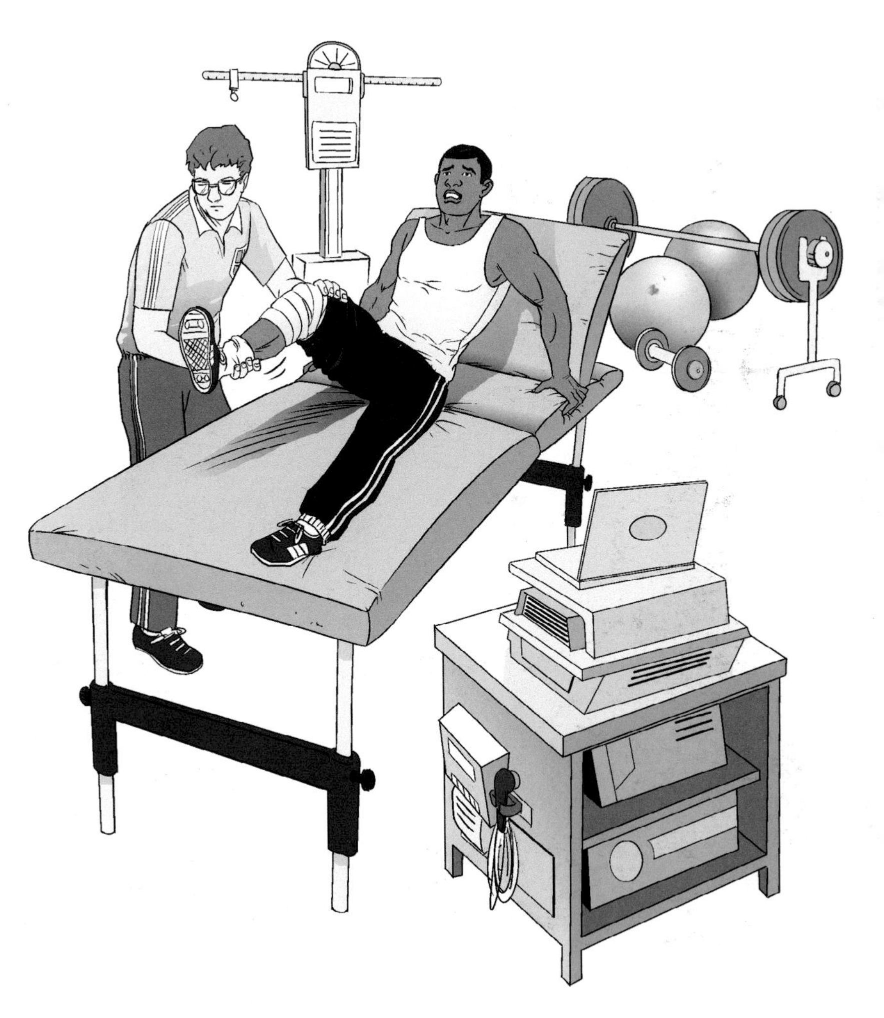

It was going to be a tough return.
It was the Cup quarter final.
Sheldon were playing away.
Ledley had to mark Ryan Strong.

Ryan was an international.
He was top scorer in the league.
But there was more.

Ledley had got his injury tackling
Ryan Strong. Ledley was worried.
What if it happened again?
What if his leg wasn't strong enough?

The game kicked off.
Ryan got the ball.
Ledley could make a tackle.
But he held back.

Ryan Strong raced away.
He shot at goal.
Ledley couldn't get near the ball.
Luckily it went over the bar.

"Come on," said Kyle. "You have to tackle."

Ledley frowned.

Ryan got the ball again.
Ledley panicked.
He slid in too fast and tripped Ryan.

The ref gave a free kick.
He gave Ledley a yellow card.
Ledley had hurt his leg.
He limped away.

Ryan took the free kick.

The ball smacked against the bar.

Ledley was scared to make
a tackle now. He might get injured.
Or he might get sent off.

The score was 0-0 at half-time.
Dave Brown, the Sheldon manager, took Ledley aside.

"You've got to get stuck in," he said.
"Sorry, boss," said Ledley.

Sheldon started the second half well.
Ryan didn't get the ball.
When it did come, it was in the air.
Ledley jumped and headed the
ball away.

Sheldon got a corner.
Ledley went upfield to attack.
Ryan went with him.
Danny took the kick.
Ledley jumped and beat Ryan
in the air.

The ball looped across the goal.
Naz headed it in.
Sheldon were ahead 1–0!
Ledley felt better now.

Sheldon had to defend attack
after attack.
Tom, Sheldon's keeper, made some
fine saves. Ledley headed balls away.
He blocked shots.

Ledley was starting to get tired.
Would his leg last out?

The match went into injury time.
The board said three minutes.
One minute passed, two…

A long ball went over the Sheldon defence. Ryan Strong ran after it. Ledley turned, but Ryan was fast. Ledley ran after him.

Ryan was in the penalty box now.
He lifted his foot to shoot…
Ledley had to make the tackle.
He had to time it just right.

He slid in and took the ball!
He had saved a certain goal!

The ref blew the final whistle.
Sheldon were in the semi-finals!

Ledley stood up slowly.

His leg was hurting, but it was okay!

Ryan Strong shook Ledley's hand.

"Well done," he said.

Ledley smiled. He had done it.
He had got through the game.
At last, he was back!

Read more stories about Sheldon Rovers.

Sheldon Rovers have made it to the Cup final. It is their manager Dave Brown's last match. Will Danny, Robby, Naz, Ledley and Tom play their best? Can they make Dave's day and win the Cup?

Danny is playing his first match for Sheldon Rovers. It is the first round of the Cup. He needs to play well to keep his place. But will nerves get the better of him?

Naz is Sheldon Rover's top scorer. He is a goal machine. But suddenly things start to go wrong. He can't score at all. He loses his place in the team. Will he ever get his goal touch back?

Tom plays in goal for Sheldon Rovers. He has a lucky horseshoe that he takes to every match. But on Cup semi-final day it goes missing. Things start to go wrong. Has Tom's luck run out?

Robby keeps getting sent off. Now he has got a three-match ban and he feels down. Can he learn to control his temper? Will he ever get back in the team?

Ledley is a defender for Sheldon Rovers. He has been out injured for months. His first game is the Cup quarter final. Will he last the game? Will his tackling be strong enough?

FOR TEACHERS

About Freestylers

Freestylers is a series of carefully levelled stories, especially geared for struggling readers of both sexes. With very low reading age and high interest age, these books are humorous, fun, up-to-the-minute and edgy. Core characters provide familiarity in all of the stories, build confidence and ease pupils from one story through to the next, accelerating reading progress.

Freestylers can be used for both guided and independent reading. To make the most of the books you can:

- Focus on making each reading session successful. Talk about the text before the pupil starts reading. Introduce the characters, the storyline and any unfamiliar vocabulary.

- Encourage the pupil to talk about the book during reading and after reading. How would they have felt if they were one of the characters playing for Sheldon Rovers? How would they have dealt with the situations that the players found themselves in?

- Talk about which parts of the story they like best and why.

For guidance, this story has been approximately measured to:

National Curriculum Level: 1B
Reading Age: 6
Book Band: Orange

ATOS: 1.5
Lexile ® Measure [confirmed]: 200L